Hello HOT DOG!

WORDS BY LILY MURRAY
PICTURES BY JARVIS

Lincoln
Children's Books

Hello, Hot Dog.

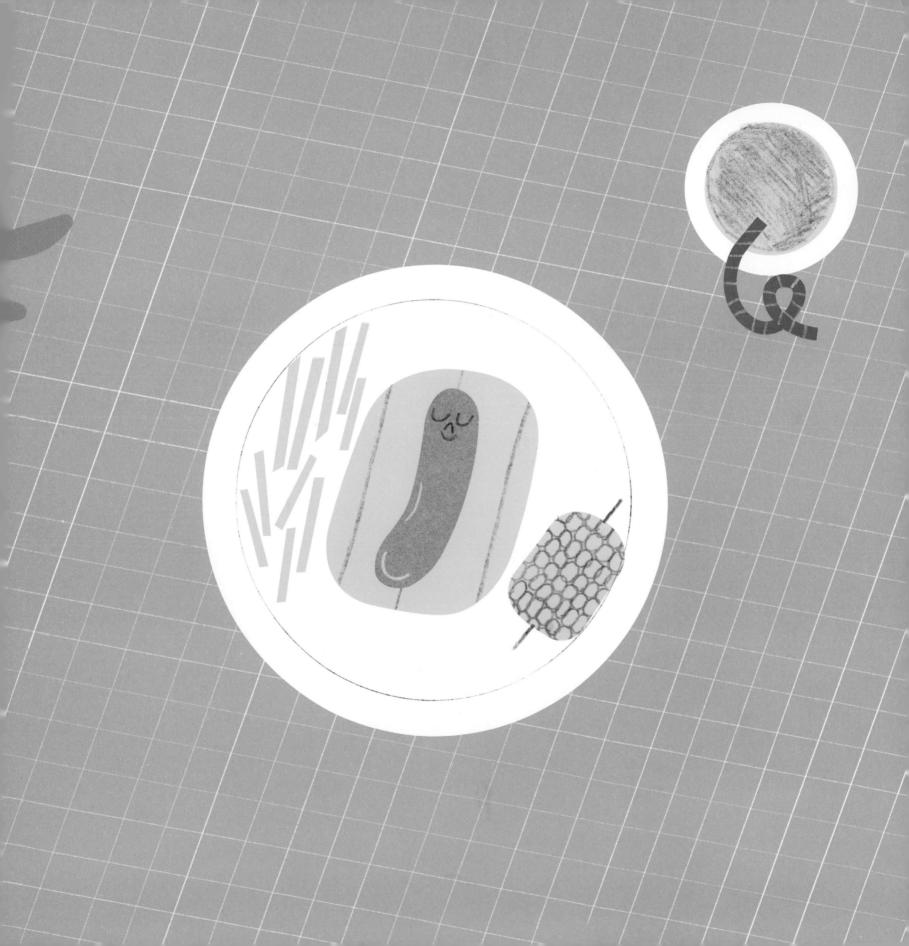

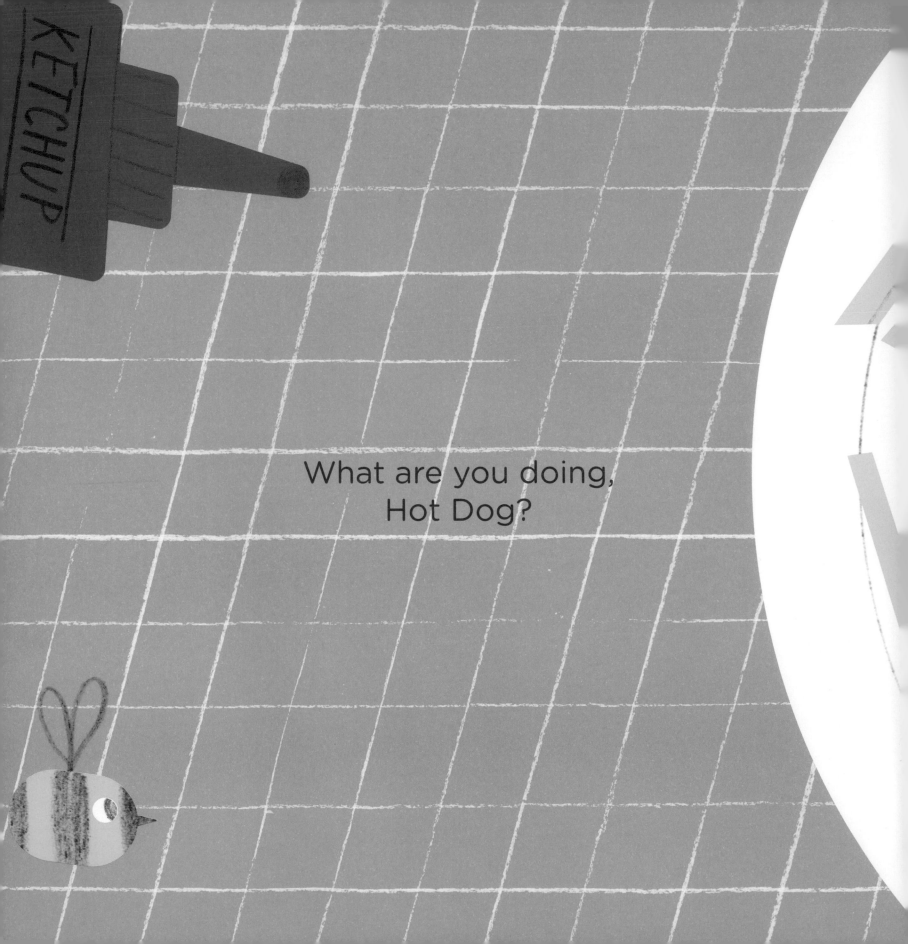

What are you doing,
Hot Dog?

It's not looking
good, is it, Hot Dog?

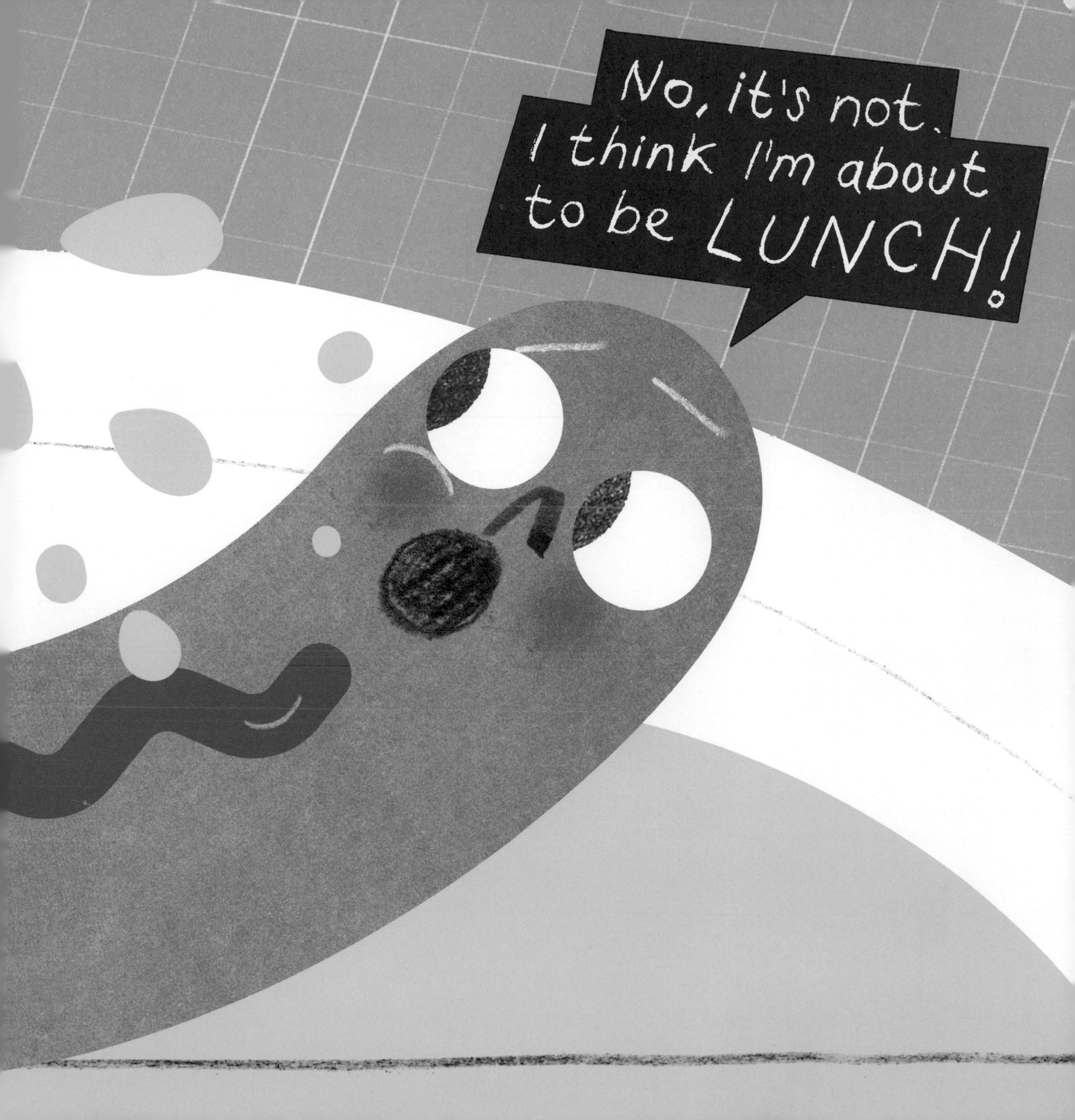
No, it's not.
I think I'm about
to be LUNCH!

Run, Hot Dog, run!

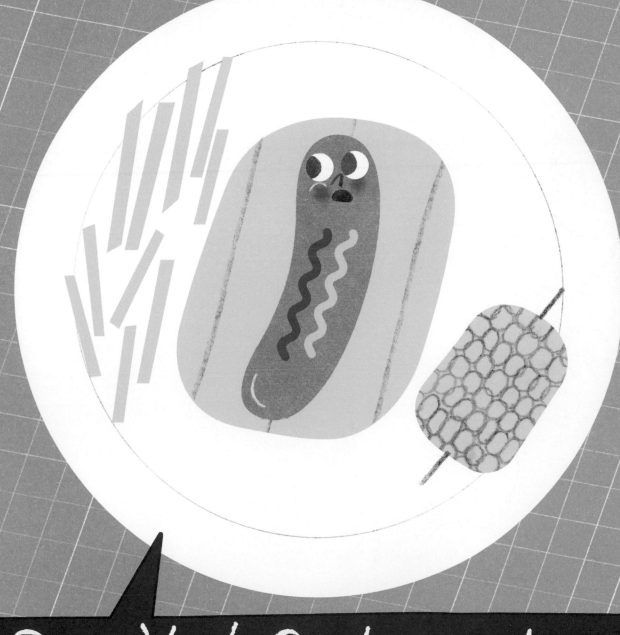

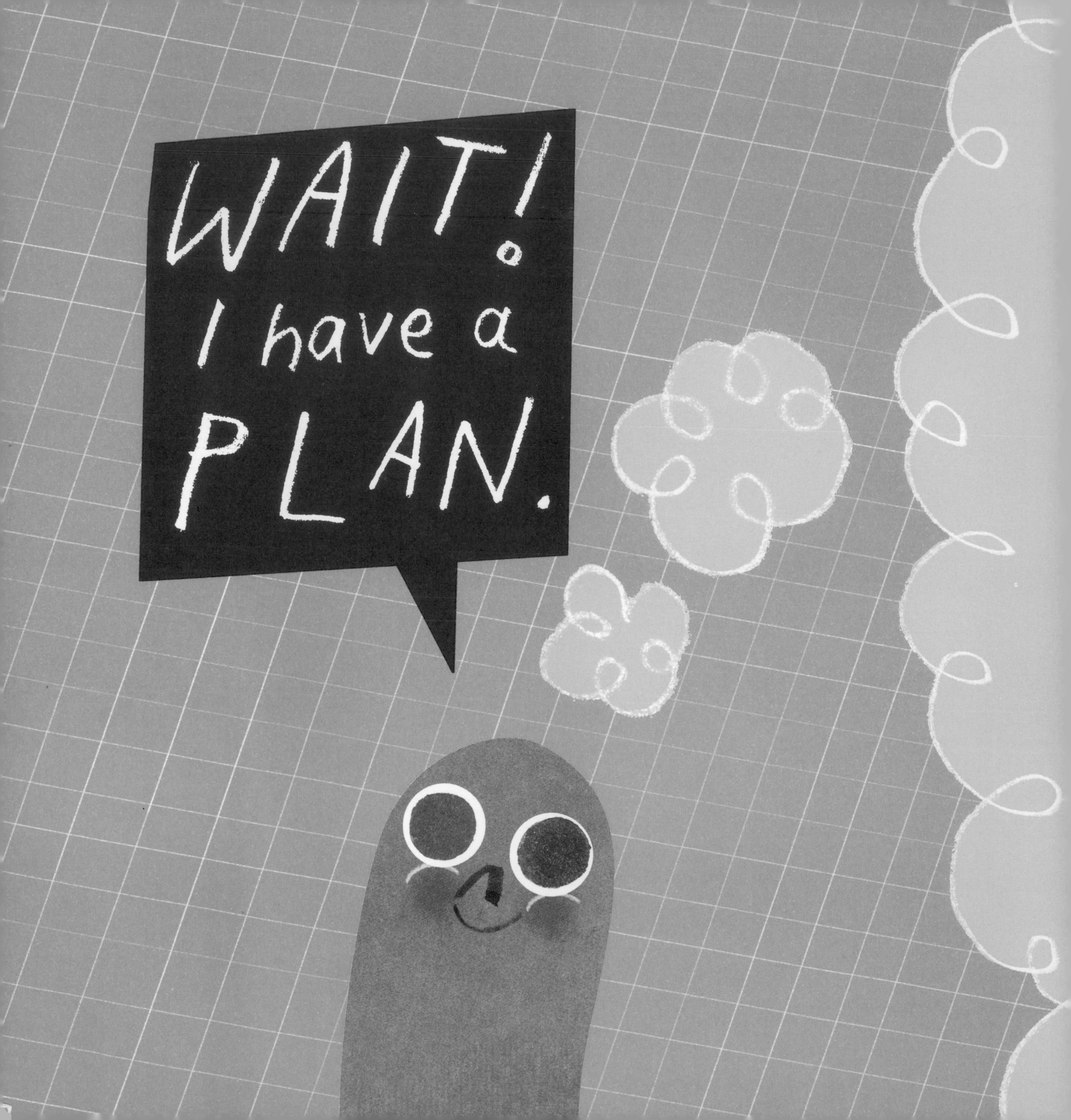
WAIT! I have a PLAN.

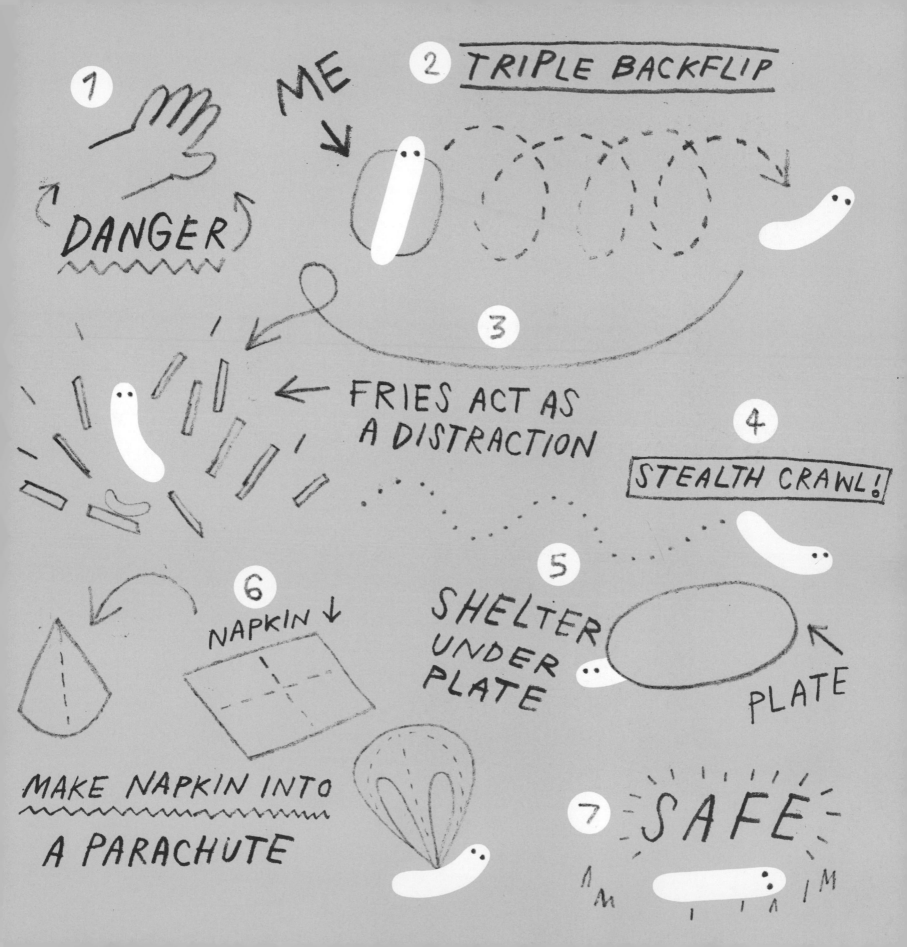

That sounds quite complicated...

WHAT was I THINKING?
I can't do a triple backflip.
This is THE END!

Don't give up, Hot Dog!
What CAN you do?

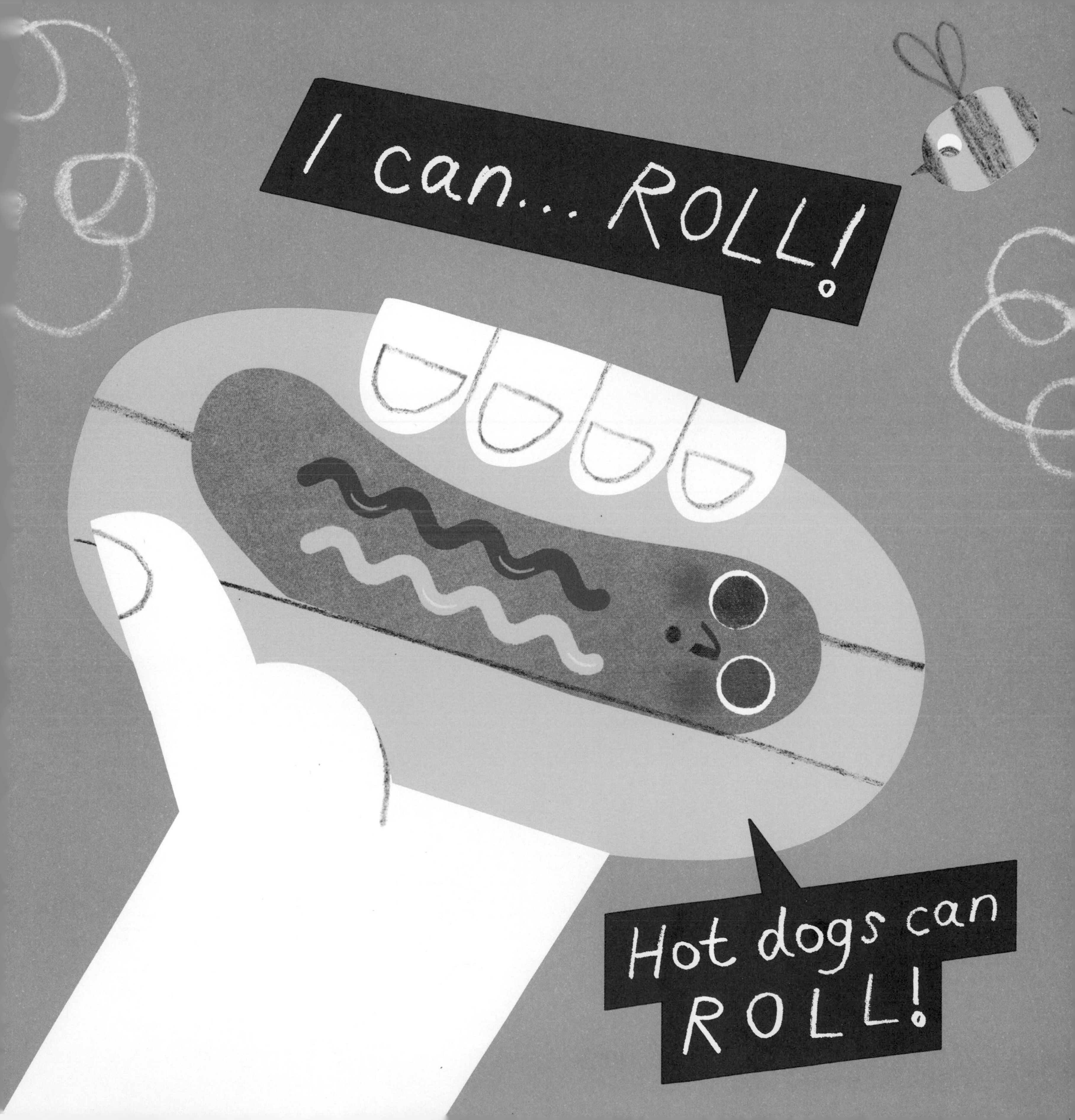
I can... ROLL!
Hot dogs can ROLL!

Well done,
Hot Dog!

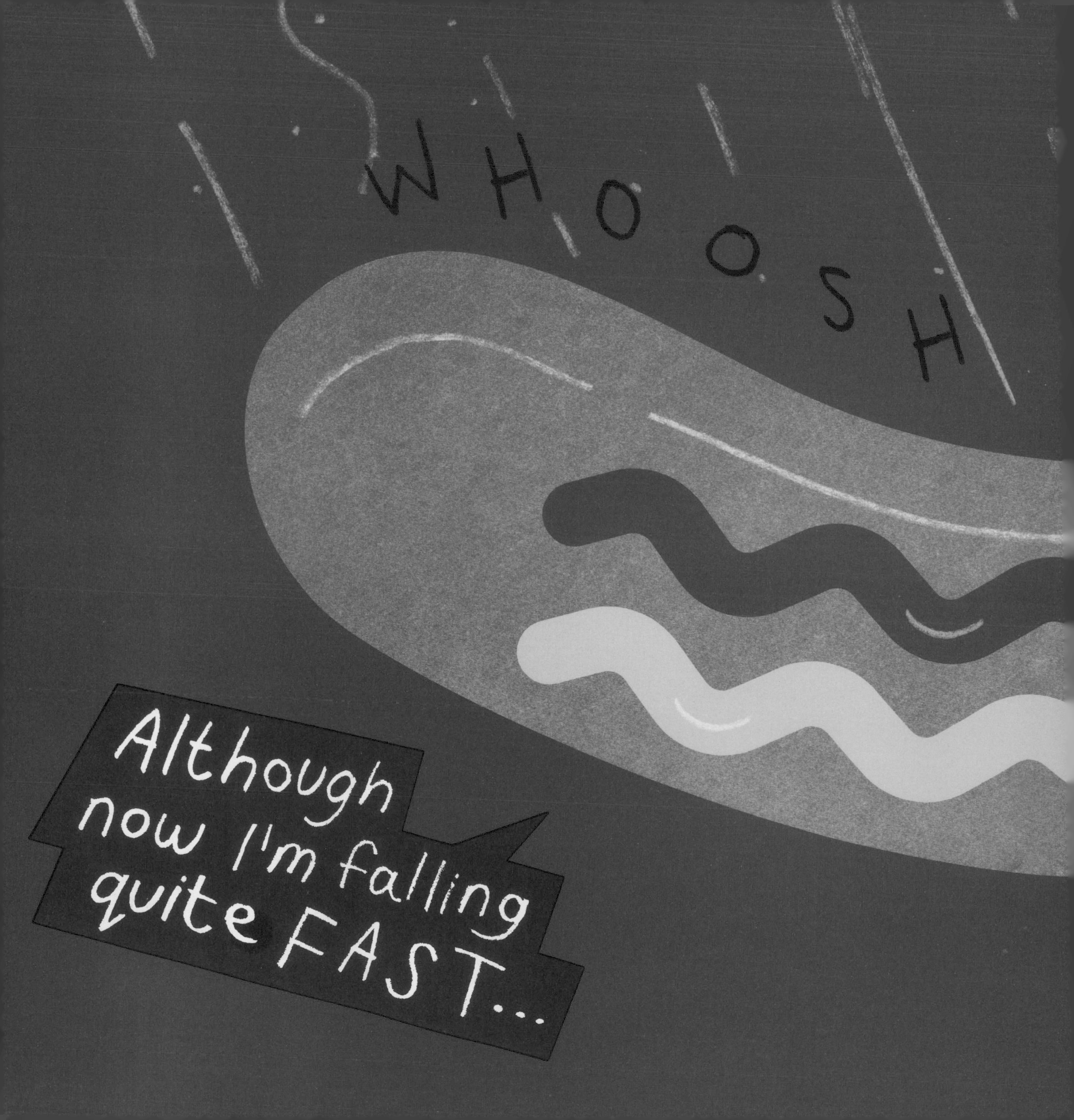
WHOOSH
Although now I'm falling quite FAST...

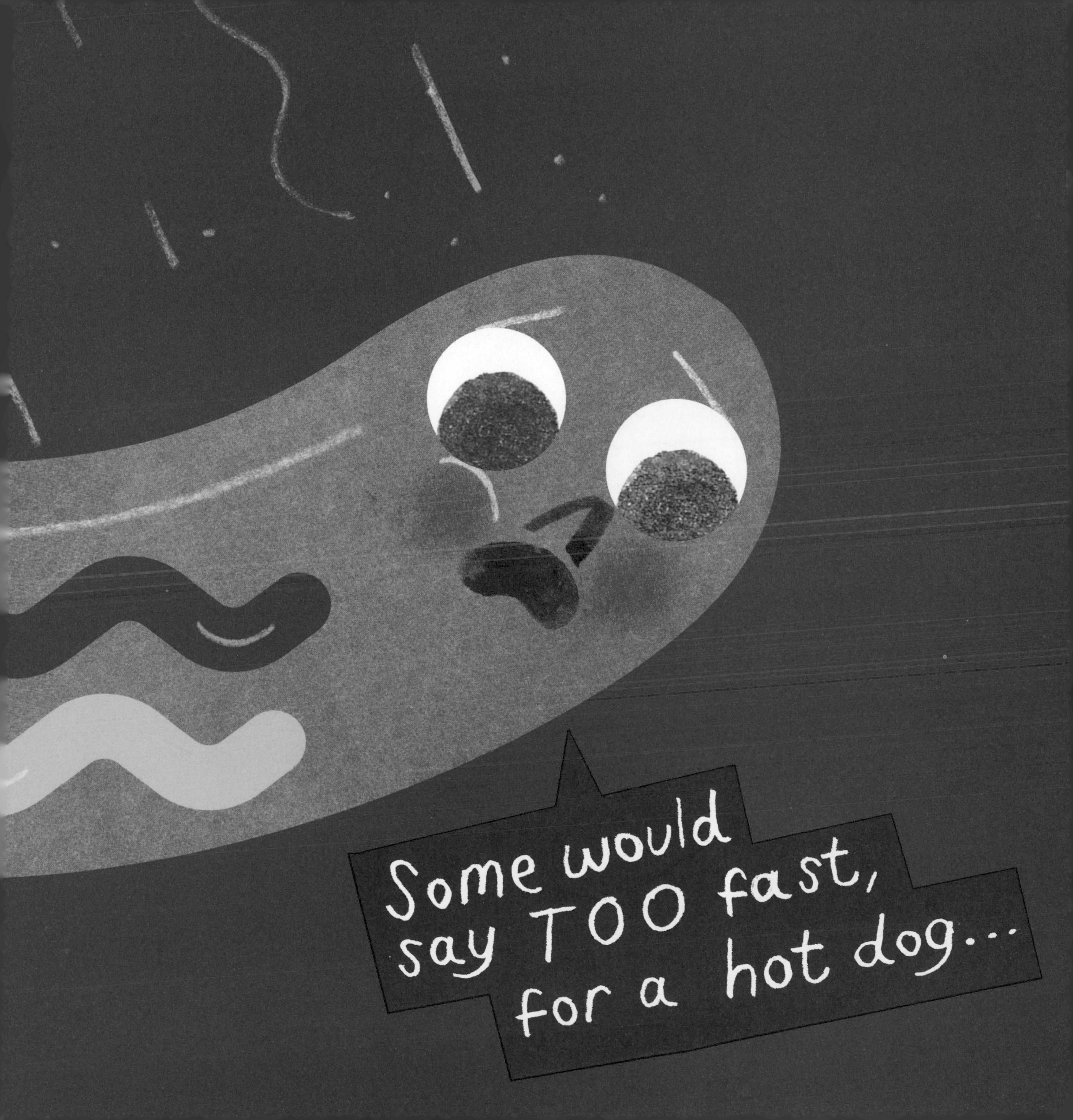
Some would say TOO fast, for a hot dog...

Are you okay,
Hot Dog?

Hot Dog?

Hello?

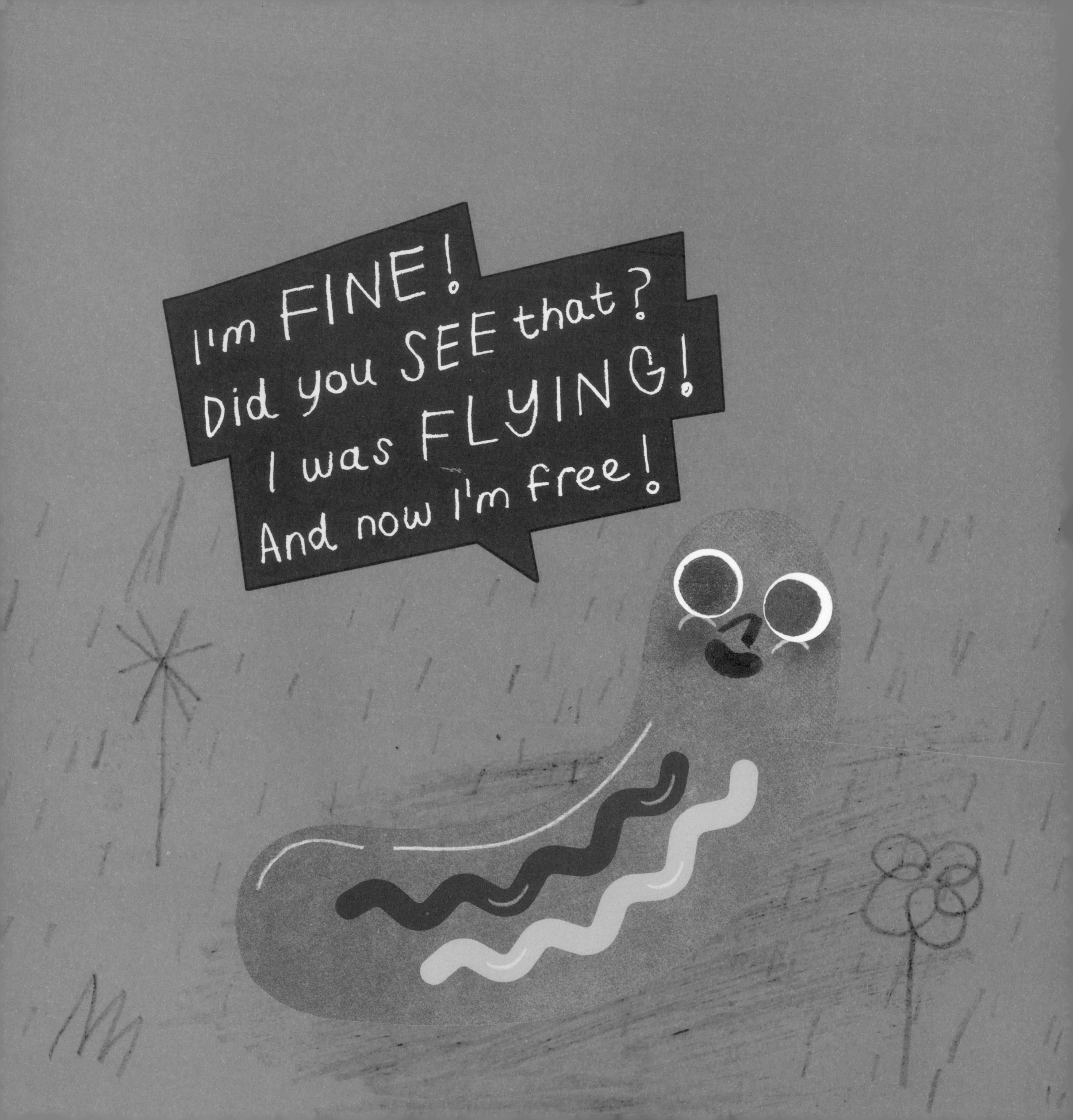
I'm FINE! Did you SEE that? I was FLYING! And now I'm free!

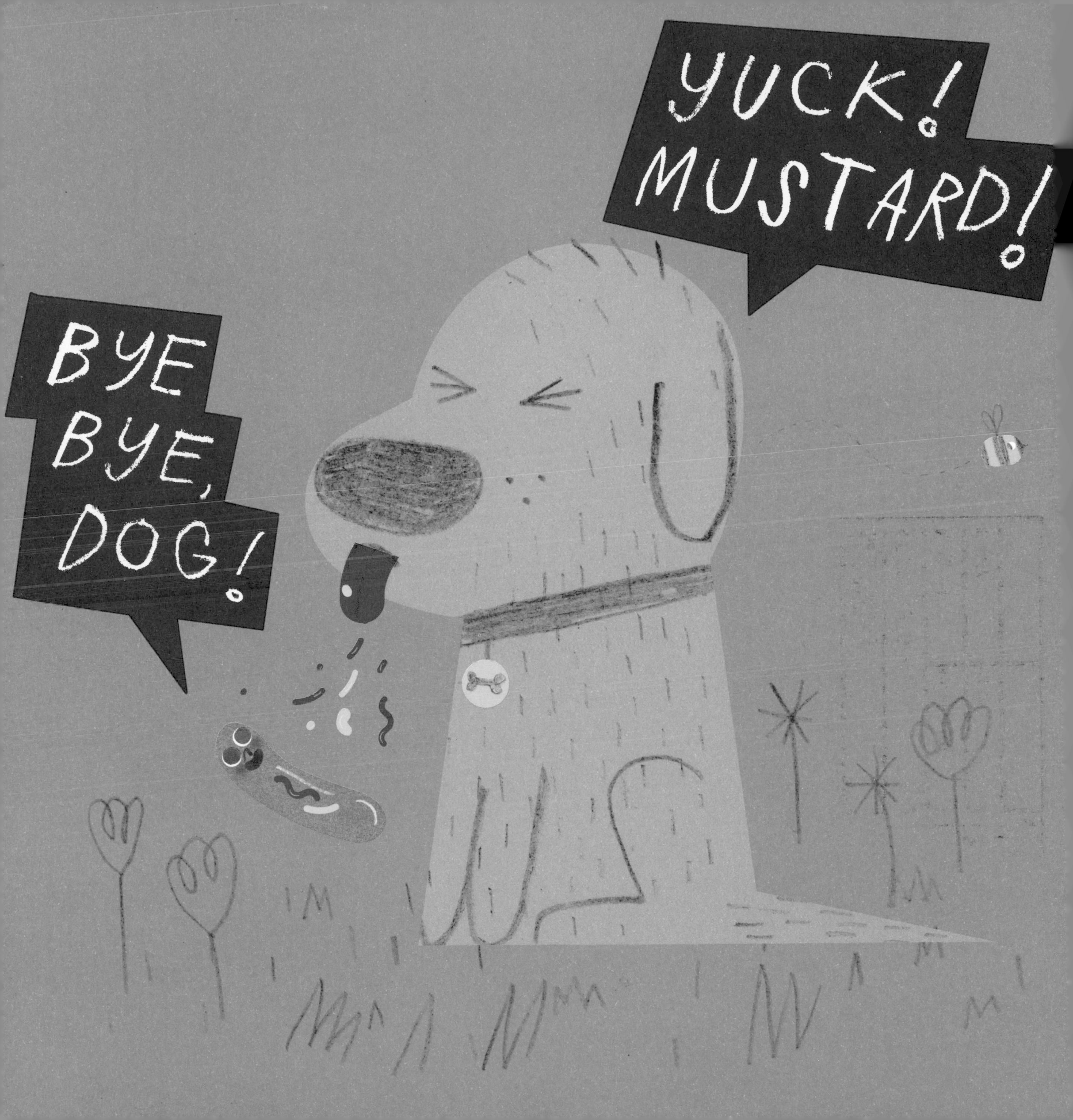
BYE BYE, DOG!
YUCK! MUSTARD!

...Hot Dog?

Hello HOT DOG!

Brimming with creative inspiration, how-to projects, and useful information to enrich your everyday life, Quarto Knows is a favourite destination for those pursuing their interests and passions. Visit our site and dig deeper with our books into your area of interest: Quarto Creates, Quarto Cooks, Quarto Homes, Quarto Lives, Quarto Drives, Quarto Explores, Quarto Gifts, or Quarto Kids.

Text © 2018 Lily Murray. Illustrations © 2018 Jarvis.

First Published in 2018 by Lincoln Children's Books,
an imprint of The Quarto Group.
The Old Brewery, 6 Blundell Street, London N7 9BH, United Kingdom.
T (0)20 7700 6700 F (0)20 7700 8066 **www.QuartoKnows.com**

A catalogue record for this book is available from the British Library.
978-1-78603-266-9
The illustrations were created with pencil and coloured digitally.
Set in Gotham Rounded
Published by Jenny Broom and Rachel Williams
Designed by Karissa Santos
Edited by Kate Davies
Production by Jenny Cundill and Kate O'Riordan
Manufactured in Dongguan, China TL112017
9 8 7 6 5 4 3 2 1

MIX
Paper from
responsible sources
FSC® C104723